GOODBYE, HOUSE

FRANK ASCH

Prentice-Hall, Inc. / Englewood Cliffs, New Jersey

Printed in Spain by Novograph, S.A., Madrid   ·J
Prentice-Hall International (UK) Limited, London
Prentice-Hall of Australia, Pty. Ltd., Sydney
Prentice-Hall Canada, Inc., Toronto
Prentice-Hall Hispanoamericana, S.A., Mexico
Prentice-Hall of India Private Ltd., New Delhi
Prentice-Hall of Japan, Inc., Tokyo
Prentice-Hall of Southeast Asia Pte. Ltd., Singapore
Whitehall Books Limited, Wellington, New Zealand
Editora Prentice-Hall do Brasil LTDA., Rio de Janeiro

10   9   8   7   6   5   4   3   2   1

Library of Congress Cataloging-in-Publication Data
Asch, Frank.
Goodbye, house.
Summary: Just before leaving with his family for the
move to their new home, Little Bear says goodbye to all
his favorite places in and around his old house.
[1. Moving, Household—Fiction. 2. Dwellings—
Fiction. 3. Bears—Fiction] I. Title.
PZ7.A778God 1986   [E]   85-19263
ISBN 0-13-360272-9

To Randy, Debbie, Serena, Emily,
Richie, and Phoebe Moon

When all the furniture was packed
in the moving van, Baby Bear said,
"Wait a minute. I think I forgot something,"
and he ran inside.

First he looked in the dining room and the kitchen. He looked in the living room, the bathroom, and in all of the bedrooms. Then he looked in the attic and the cellar. He looked everywhere.

But the house was empty.

"Did you find what you were looking for?" asked
Mama Bear.

"No, Mama," said Baby Bear, "the house is empty."

"So you think the house is empty," said Papa Bear.

"Yes," said Baby Bear with a sigh,

"everything we own is in the van."

"What about the memories?" said Papa Bear.

"I remember where my chair used to go," said Mama.

"My chair was right there," said Papa Bear.

"And mine was right here," said Baby Bear.

For a moment everything in the house looked just

as it was before, but soon...

...it all...

. . . faded away.

"Come on," said Papa Bear, "let's say goodbye."
And he picked up Baby Bear
and carried him from room to room.

They said goodbye to the dining room...

and the stairs.

They said goodbye to the bedrooms and the halls,

the ceilings and the walls.

They said goodbye to the attic...

...and the cellar.

They said goodbye to the floors, the doors, the windows, and the kitchen sink. And when they had said goodbye to everything in the back yard...

they locked the front door...

and said goodbye to the whole house.

Then they climbed into the moving van

and drove away.

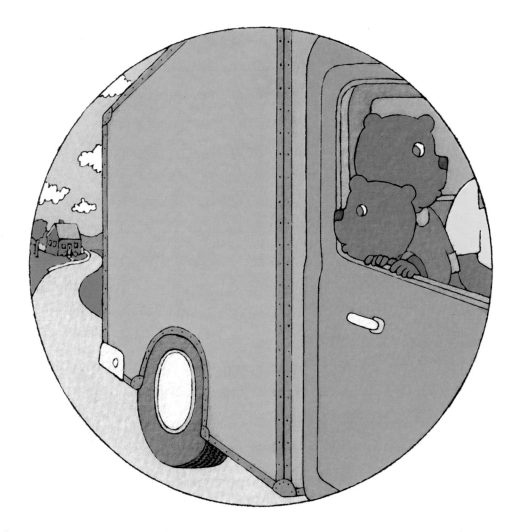

And as they drove away, Baby Bear said,
"That's what I forgot.
I forgot to say goodbye."